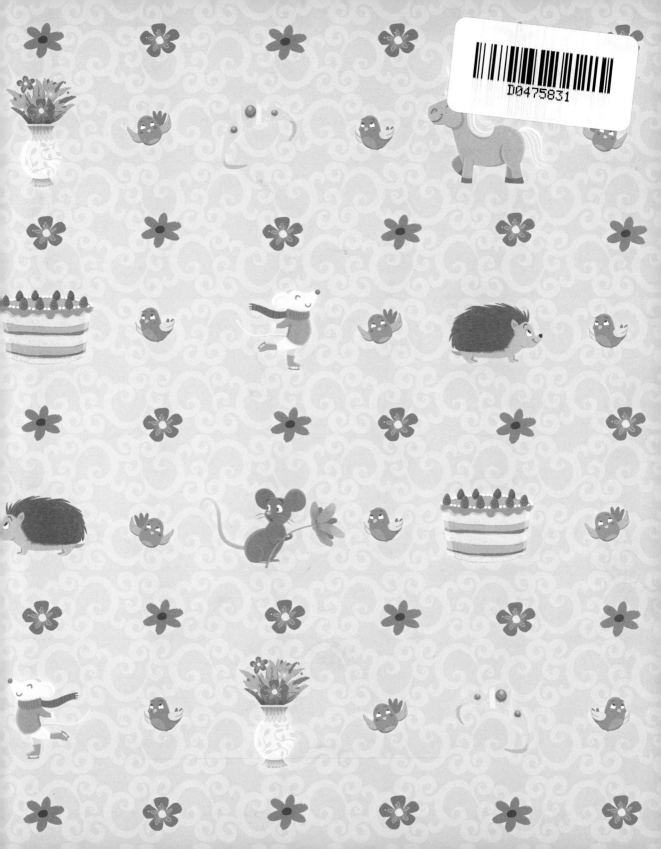

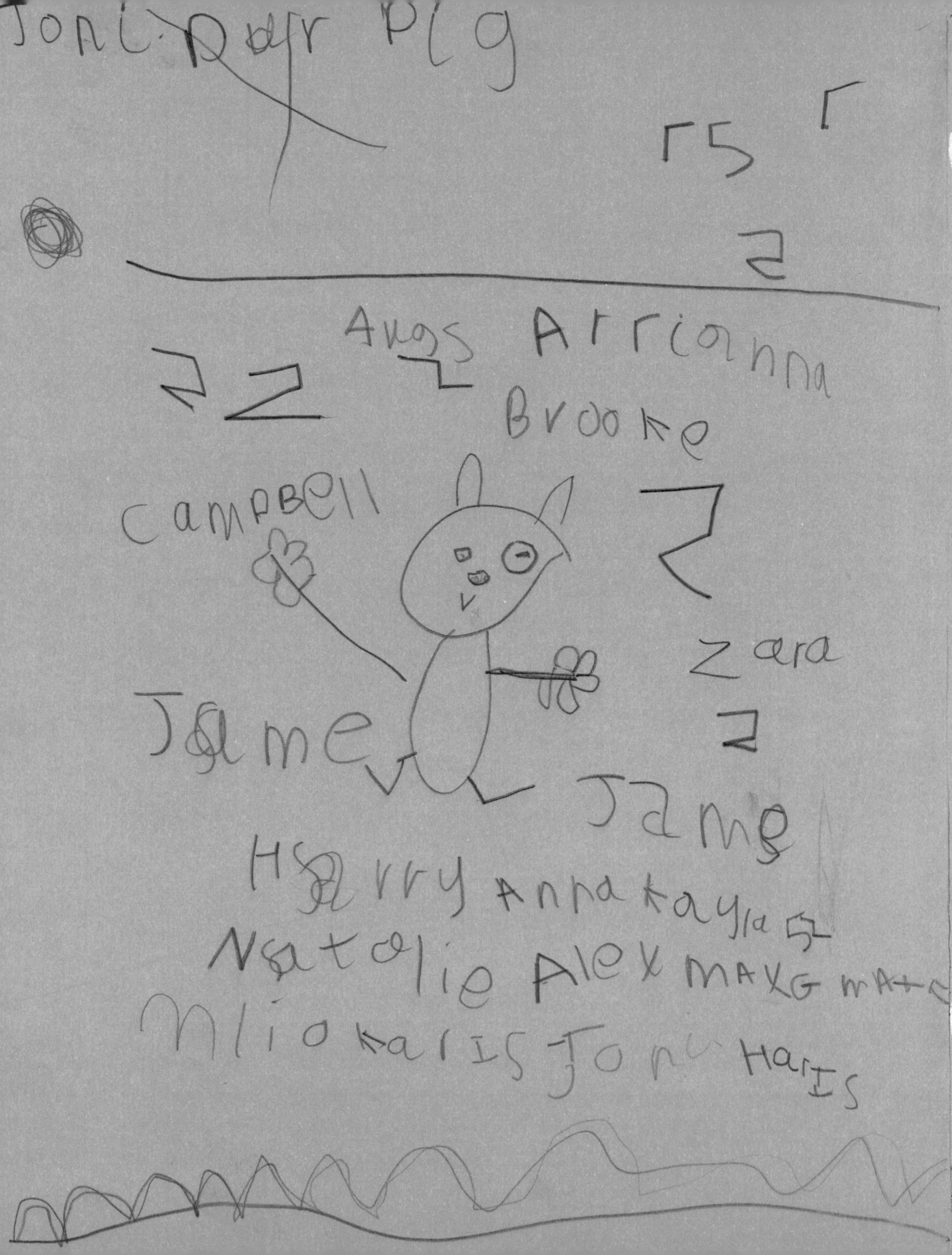

Jonl par pig

r5 r

2

N N

Augs Arrianna

Brooke

Campbell

Zara

N

Jame

Jame

Hsarry Anna kayla S

Natalie Alex Maxg mate

nlio kaI IS Jone HaIIS

This igloo book belongs to:

Contents

igloobooks

Published in 2017
by Igloo Books Ltd, Cottage Farm, Sywell, NN6 0BJ
www.igloobooks.com

Copyright © 2017 Igloo Books Ltd

Illustrated by Heather Burns
Additional colour by Sara Foresti
Written by Xanna Chown and Melanie Joyce

Designed by Katie Messenger
Edited by Natalia Boileau

STA002 0617
2 4 6 8 10 9 7 5 3 1
ISBN 978-1-78557-379-8

Printed and manufactured in China

5 Minute Tales

Magical Stories

igloobooks

Sunshine and Snow

Fairy twins, Daisy and Crystal, were having a joint party. They put up decorations, changed into sparkly dresses and admired the **delicious** unicorn cake their mum had made.

But there was just one thing they couldn't agree on, which theme would be best for the party?

I want a **summer** picnic party with ice cream!

said Daisy.

I want a **winter** wonderland party with snowmen!

said Crystal.

Just as the guests started to arrive, the twins **swished** their wands at exactly the same time.

The guests gasped to see half the garden **sparkling** with snow, while the other half **dazzled** with sunshine.

Some guests waved their wands to make woolly hats, while others magicked up sun hats and summer dresses.

The friends wanted to play with both
twins, but they got in a terrible muddle.

Their thick coats were too **warm** for the summer picnic...

We're too **hot!**

said Lola.

... and their summer dresses made them **shiver** in the snow.

We're **freezing!**

said Bluebell.

No one wanted ice cream at the winter party,
or hot chocolate at the summer one. Even worse, one half
of the unicorn cake **melted**, while the other half **froze.**

Suddenly, Daisy tripped, and her bowl of summer berries flew through the air. **Splat!** Two juicy berries landed on Crystal's snowman.

They look like ears.

said Daisy, giggling.

Crystal and Daisy looked at one another and burst out laughing.

Crystal and Daisy looked around at the muddled garden.

We've made a mess of this, haven't we?

said Crystal.

Let's turn the weather back to normal.

replied Daisy.

The twins **swished** their wands together and in a flash of sparkles, the hot sunshine and freezing snow **disappeared**.

Just then, a bright beautiful rainbow **arched** across the sky. Crystal and Daisy hugged one another and were glad to be friends again.

Sharing this party with you is the most **important** thing.

said Daisy.

Whatever the weather!

added Crystal.

The Perfect Parade

Princess Sapphire watched the other princesses trotting around on their unicorns, as they rehearsed for the royal parade. It looked like so much fun, if only she had her **own** unicorn to ride.

You can put up the parade decorations instead, Sapphire.

said one princess, giggling.

It's not fair!

said Sapphire,
sadly.

As Sapphire went to fetch
the glittery decorations,
she realised that someone
had already taken them.

Where have all the
decorations gone?

gasped Sapphire.

Just then, Sapphire noticed some unusual footprints.
Curious, she followed them into the royal gardens.

Sapphire jumped as a loud **sneeze** and
a **puff** of smoke came from behind a tree.

Creeping closer, she saw a little dragon tangled up in twinkly fairy lights, his nose twitching with glitter.

Hey! Give us our decorations back!

demanded Sapphire.

I can't, I'm **stuck!**

wailed the dragon.

I'm sorry I took the decorations. People think that dragons are **fierce**. I thought I'd look less scary if I **sparkled**.

said the dragon, sadly.

Sapphire felt sorry for the dragon and quickly untangled him. **"You just need a little help,"** she said

16

Carefully, Sapphire looped the glittering lights around the dragon's neck and **sprinkled** glitter on his tail. Suddenly, she heard **tinkling** music coming from the royal town.

The royal parade is starting!

exclaimed Sapphire.

Sapphire hopped on the dragon's back. With a **whoosh,**
they flew up to join the parade. The other princesses were
so amazed to see a sparkly dragon that they couldn't
wait to meet him afterwards.

This has
been the most
perfect parade!

cheered Sapphire.

The Mermaid Party

Deep under the sparkling waves, mermaid sisters, Coral and Pearl, swam off to the deep sea disco.

Wait for me!

cried their little sister, Marina.

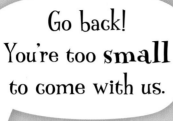

Go back!
You're too **small**
to come with us.

said Pearl.

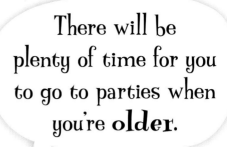

There will be
plenty of time for you
to go to parties when
you're **older**.

said Marina's mum.

"For now, you must stay
here where you're safe and
play with the seahorses,"
she added, giving Marina
a big cuddle.

21

But when her mum wasn't looking, Marina slid her
best seashell clip in her hair and swished her tail.

Before she knew it, she was beyond the
beautiful reef and out into the big, blue sea.

Far ahead, Marina could just see the **shimmer** of her sisters' tails. She swam and swam to try to catch up, but their tails disappeared into the distance. Soon, Marina realised that she was all alone.

I'll just rest for a while on this rock.

she said.

Suddenly, the rock began to move, and Marina realised it wasn't a rock at all. It was a **huge** whale! Up and up they went.

Look, Mummy! It's a mermaid!

said a little boy.

Whoosh!

A huge spray of water sent Marina **somersaulting** through the air above the waves. Then down, down she came...

Splosh!

With a crash, Marina splashed back into the sea and tumbled through a **whirling** shoal of silver fish.

Marina felt very **dizzy.** As quickly as they appeared, the shoal of silver fish hurried away.

Why were those silly fish in such a rush?

huffed Marina.

Suddenly, through the rippling water, Marina saw a mean, hungry **swordfish** swimming straight towards her.

Thinking quickly, Marina **darted** into a dark sea cave to hide.
The fierce fish soon gave up looking for her and swam away.

But just when Marina thought she was safe, a grumpy octopus
wound his long **wiggly** tentacles around her tail, trapping her.

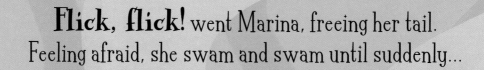

Flick, flick! went Marina, freeing her tail.
Feeling afraid, she swam and swam until suddenly...

...**Argh!**

The octopus has **caught** me!

she cried.

But it wasn't the octopus
at all, it was her sisters.

We knew you'd
follow us.

they sighed.

Marina was so happy to see her sisters and even happier
still when they had their very own mermaid party at home.

The Unhappy Princess

Princess Mia lived in a beautiful palace filled with toys, games and sparkling dresses.

I should be the happiest princess in the world.

she sighed.

But no matter how many toys she had, she didn't feel happy at all.

One day, Mia found a **magic** gold coin that
she had never seen before in the palace garden.

I wish I knew
what would make
me happy.

she whispered.

Then she
dropped the coin
into the sparkling
fountain and sighed.

Suddenly, a spiral of sparkles **whooshed**
past her and a **shining** unicorn appeared.

Climb on my back and hold on tight.

said the unicorn.

Then the unicorn **flapped** his sparkling wings and lifted into the air. The wind whipped Mia's hair loose and sent her tiara flying.

Up, up they flew, over fields and trees until
the palace was a speck in the distance.

The unicorn landed where three children were playing and shrieking
with laughter. When they saw Mia, they stopped and bowed.

"Please don't stop, it looks such fun," said Mia.

It is! Would you like to play chase with us?

said the girl, kindly.

Mia joined the fun at once. She jumped, skipped, tumbled and slipped right into a **squelchy** mud patch, but she was laughing too much to care.

34

After the game, the children shared their picnic
with Mia, and even gave the unicorn an apple.

Soon, the unicorn stretched his beautiful wings and told Mia that it was time to leave.

I have hundreds of toys at home, but no one to play with.

she said, sadly.

Mia suddenly realised what would make her happy.

Mia invited the children to play at her palace. The children hopped on the unicorn's back and **whooshed** through the sky. Before long, they arrived at the palace grounds.

Now I'm the **happiest** princess in the world.

said Mia, with the biggest smile.

The Elf Prince

It was the day of the elf prince's visit and the fairy queen and her helpers were busy dusting and polishing everything in sight.

The fairies gave everything an extra sprinkling of fairy dust, even the royal swans. But when the elf prince arrived, he walked around with his nose in the air.

Blue swans? How **boring.** The ones at home are every colour of the rainbow.

said the prince, snootily.

Inside the palace, the prince was even ruder.

Call these flowers? The ones at home can sing and dance.

he sniggered.

The fairies offered him one of the cupcakes the palace chef had been busy baking all morning.

No, no, no! I only eat cakes made with diamond dust.

he said.

All day, the prince moaned and complained, but he was rudest of all at the royal banquet. As one fairy served the soup, he **sighed** very loudly.

Fairy wings are so annoying. All this flapping is making my food go cold.

he groaned.

The fairies were upset by the prince's harsh words, but were too polite to say anything. Suddenly, there was a loud **rumble** outside as clouds gathered over the palace.

Fairyland storms can be very dangerous. We must all stay inside where it's safe.

warned the fairy queen.

It's only rain. Storms are much stronger at home.

grumbled the prince.

Suddenly, a fierce wind blew and threw the prince to the floor, as the door **slammed** shut behind him.

Help!

he cried.

Lightning **flashed** and thunder **crashed**. The prince tried to open the door, but it was stuck. Failing, he huddled up and began to sob.

I want my mummy!

he wailed.

The fairies raced out of the banqueting hall,
down the stairs and into the garden.

We'll save him!

they cried.

The rain was
falling so fast they could
hardly beat their wings, but
they managed to struggle into the air.

The determined little fairies battled through
the storm to the balcony, where they found the prince.

Hold on tight!

they shouted.

The fairies carried the **shivering** prince safely down to the
castle where the fairy queen was waiting with warm blankets.

The soaking prince was very grateful.

Thank goodness for fairy wings. I'm sorry I was rude about them, and for all my boasting.

he said, feeling embarrassed.

The fairies forgave him at once.

One of the fairies handed the elf prince a mug
of creamy hot chocolate and he took a sip.

This tastes awful...

he said.

Then the elf prince grinned at the fairies' shocked faces.

... Awfully good!
It's even better than the
hot chocolate at home.

he added.